Other Ashridge Bears books you will enjoy

Ashridge Christmas
Birthday Surprise
Fun on the Pond
Visitors to Stay
Winter's Coming

Text © Margaret Carter 1993
Illustrations © Richard Fowler 1993
First published 1993 by
Campbell Books
This edition published 1995 by
Campbell Books
12 Half Moon Court · London EC1A 7HE
Printed in Great Britain by Cambus Litho Ltd

ISBN 1 85292 255 9 (paperback)

Winter's Coming

Margaret Carter
Richard Fowler

CAMPBELL BOOKS

— the children played very happily in the forest —

Winter's coming

In the middle of the great forest called Ashridge there once lived a family of bears. There was a father, a mother, two boys – Tim and George – and the baby, who was called Daisy.

During summer the children played very happily in the forest but when the leaves on the trees turned from green to red and yellow, they knew winter was coming.

'We must get ready for the cold weather,'
Mother Bear would say.

Then she would make the children try on
their wellies to see that they didn't
let in water, and she would try on their
woolly hats to see if they still fitted.

Mostly they didn't, of course, and
very funny they looked too!

'Oh dear!' Mother Bear would say.

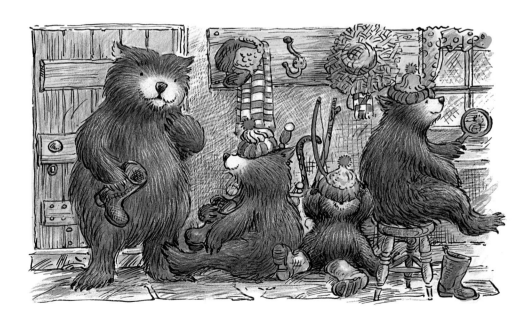

But what the children liked best of all
was helping father to collect wood for
the winter fires.

Every day they would ask, 'Shall we get
the wood today, father?' And every day
he would reply, 'Soon, children, soon!'

And then one morning, after breakfast, he
put down his newspaper, looked out of the
window and said, 'I think we'll see how much
wood there is left in the shed.'

'Hooray!' cried both boys together.

Now the shed was very dark inside and a bit scary. At first they couldn't see anything and then they heard a very faint noise . . . *rustle, rustle,* it went.

'Help!' said George. 'Goodness!' said Tim and in case it was something quite dreadful they both got behind father.

Two bright eyes were shining through the darkness. Slowly a face grew round the eyes. It was a dormouse!

'Why Dormouse,' said George, 'whatever
are you doing here?' 'I'm making my winter
nest,' yawned Dormouse. 'Soon I shall curl
myself into a ball, chin on tummy, very warm
and cosy and there I'll sleep until the
daffodils are blooming.'

And with a last yawn he scampered off.

Father had been looking at the logs left
from last year. 'We'll need a lot more than
these,' he said. 'Get the sledge out, boys.'

'And here's your picnic,' called mother.

They ate every scrap and shared the last crumbs with the birds.

As Daisy couldn't walk very fast, they gave her a ride on the sledge and very soon they came to a great beech tree that had fallen in the storms. 'Just right for us,' said father and while he chopped at the branches the boys piled the logs on the sledge. Daisy sat and watched them.

For some time they all worked very hard and soon the sledge was almost full.

At last father stopped, mopping his brow. 'Let's have our picnic,' he said.

The food was delicious: hot soup, buns and sausages, apples and honey cakes. They ate every scrap and shared the last crumbs with the birds.

Then suddenly, 'Ooo!' cried Daisy.

She was rubbing her head and pointing to an acorn in the grass.

'It must have fallen from the tree,' said Tim. 'But Daisy, it can't have hurt you at all – it's very small.'

'Back to work, boys,' said father, but George stayed behind, looking up at the tree. A pair of bright eyes was looking down at him. 'You threw that nut, Squirrel,' he whispered. 'But I won't tell!' And he was smiling as he ran to join the others.

Naughty George

George was getting very tired of helping his father and brother to collect wood for their winter fires.

'Isn't it time to go home yet?' he asked, rather sadly.

'Nearly,' said Father Bear. 'I just want to finish chopping this last branch.'

'If you'd help a bit more,' grumbled Tim, 'we could get home sooner.'

But George didn't answer. He had already wandered away into the forest.

Soon he came to the big oak tree under which they had eaten their picnic. 'I wonder if that squirrel who threw the acorn at Daisy is still there?' he thought.

At that moment, *plop!* There was an acorn on the grass in front of him. He looked up and staring down at him was a little grey face with twinkly eyes.

'Wait for me, Squirrel,' he called. 'I'm coming up there as well.' And he began to climb the tree.

Up and up through the branches he went. At last, with one last puff, he reached the squirrel.

'You can't climb trees as quickly as I can,' said Squirrel. 'No,' agreed George, 'but I can do other things.' 'What sort of things?' asked the squirrel, very interested.

George thought. 'I can carry logs of wood,' he said at last. 'Well,' said the squirrel, 'will you help me carry these acorns to my nest?' 'Certainly,' said George.

'Why are you gathering so many acorns?'
George wanted to know.

'It's food for my winter larder,' was the
reply. 'I put a nice little pile of acorns
in a safe place, then in winter I curl up
in my warm nest – which is called a drey – and
I sleep and sleep. But if I should wake up
and feel I need a snack, then I know just where
to find something tasty.'

But George wasn't really listening. He was staring down through the branches. 'Look, there's my sister, Daisy. Shall we drop acorns on her to make her laugh?'

So they did. But Daisy didn't laugh at all. In fact, 'Ooh Ooh!' she shrieked in alarm.

'George!' called father. 'I know you're up there. Come down at once!'

Two small faces – one grey and one brown – were looking down from the tree. 'Sorry, Daisy,' said George but he was still laughing.

George began to climb down the tree
and then he suddenly stopped. 'Father,'
he called, 'I can see some lovely blackberries!
Can we go and pick them for mother?'

'Oh yes, please,' said Tim. 'Then we can
have blackberry pie!'

'A good idea,' said father. 'Show us
the way, George.'

George led the way to where he had seen
the blackberries. 'There, look!' he said.
There they were – shining and black and
very beautiful.

'Oh I do so love blackberries,' cried Tim
and he took a great mouthful of them. But
then, 'Oh they're horrible,' he cried. 'All
sour and horrible!' and his face was
screwed up like a brown paper bag.

George laughed so much he had to sit
down. 'You need to put sugar with
them,' he said. 'Poor Tim!'

George led the way to where he had seen the blackberries.

They all picked the blackberries and soon they had so many that the picnic basket was quite full.

'Time to go home,' said father. 'We've done a good day's work and you've all helped me very much.'

Tim and George carried the basket between them and because there was no room for Daisy on the sledge, she had a ride on father's shoulders, holding very tightly to his ears.

They walked home rather slowly because they were all tired, until in the distance they saw lights shining through the shadows.

'It's our house,' said Tim. 'And there's mother waiting for us,' said George.

But Daisy said nothing. She was fast asleep, curled up like a small brown scarf round father's neck.

Home for tea

Mother Bear was delighted with the
blackberries the children had picked.

'I shall be able to make lots of pies
with these,' she said. 'Thank you very
much, boys. Now if you would just put the
logs in the shed you could have your bath
afterwards.'

'When do we have something to eat?'
asked George, anxiously. 'When you've had
your bath,' said mother very firmly.

Now the boys had quite forgotten that
the shed was a bit scary but as soon as
they got to the door, they remembered.

'It's very dark in there,' said George,
peering in. 'Hm,' said Tim, 'why don't we
just stand in the doorway and throw the
logs in – then we needn't gg . . go right in.'

They threw in two logs then George said
'Stop it, Tim.' 'Stop what?' asked Tim. 'I'm
not doing anything.' 'You're tickling my
cheek,' growled George. 'No I'm not,'said Tim.

'Well something is,' shrieked George – and
they both got stuck in the doorway, trying
to get out.

They held each other for comfort and
stared into the darkness.

'I felt something,' whispered George.
'It was terrible – sort of fluttery and
very, very tickly . . .'

'It was only me,' said a very small voice.

Dangling in the doorway, swinging on
a thread, was a rather large spider.

'Oh Spider,' sighed George, 'you
really frightened me!'

'Sorry I'm sure,' giggled the spider. 'I was just spinning my web and swinging about and I suppose I touched your cheek by mistake. Quite by mistake of course!'

But George wasn't sure. He thought it quite possible that Spider had tickled him on purpose, especially as he heard him giggling as he scuttled away.

'I can't stand any more frights,' said Tim. As quickly as they could they threw the rest of the logs into the shed.

'Everyone's getting ready for winter,' said George. 'Dormouse is building a nest, Squirrel is gathering acorns and we're collecting wood.'

Just then they heard father calling. 'Time for your bath, boys,' he said.

'Thank goodness,' they both said and they ran back to the house as fast as their legs would carry them.

The bathroom was warm and steamy. Tim got in the bath then George squirted in the bubble bath. But he squirted so much that the bubbles floated up to the ceiling where they burst with soft little plops.

When George got in with Tim they played at submarines. This meant lying flat with just your nose sticking up and tickling each other's toes under water.

'That's funny,' said George, after a while, 'there's not much water in the bath.' 'That's because most of it is on the floor,' Tim said.

'Tea's ready,' called mother from downstairs.

'Hooray!' said George and he got out of the bath so quickly that, *crash!* he slipped on the wet floor and got his head stuck in the waste paper basket.

Well, of course, Tim laughed and laughed.

– 'there's not much water in the bath' –

'Get me out of here,' called George.
'I'm stuck!'

Tim gave the basket a good tug. It came off George's head so suddenly that now it was Tim's turn to sit down – and George's turn to laugh.

'What's going on up here?' asked father, putting his head round the door. 'Oh boys, boys, what a *mess*! Now you can just clear it all up!'

They did their best. They mopped away
(and sometimes slapped each other with wet
cloths when father wasn't looking) and soon
the bathroom was tidy – almost.

'That's better,' said father. 'Now at last
we can go downstairs and have our tea.'

In front of a warm fire, the table was laid
for tea. There were boiled eggs and brown toast,
and small iced buns with cherries on top.

And in each place there was a new woolly hat –
red for Tim, blue for George and a stripy one
for Daisy made with the bits left over.

'I made them this afternoon,' said mother,
'so that your heads will be warm in winter.'

They all liked their hats so much that they
put them on at once and wore them while
they were having tea.

Their hard work in the forest had made
them very hungry and soon all the plates
on the table were empty.

'I hope you've left room for something special,' said mother. She went into the kitchen and came back carrying something very carefully. On to the table she put the most delicious looking pie. It was brown and crusty and shining with sugar.

'I made it with the blackberries you picked for me,' she said.

When the pie dish was empty and the last crusty bits scraped out (it was Tim's turn to scrape the dish) they pulled their chairs closer to the fire and father read them their bedtime story.

But the fire was so warm and their tummies so full and father's voice was so deep and rumbling – just like an old bee buzzing among summer flowers – that soon their heads began to nod. 'They're fast asleep,' said mother.

They carried them upstairs and tucked them into bed and soon there was no sound except the soft breathing of three small bears, now fast asleep – and even in their sleep they would know that when the white snows of winter covered the great wood they would be safe and warm, all together, in their own cosy home.

LIFE IN
ANCIENT
ATHENS

JANE SHUTER

Heinemann
LIBRARY

www.heinemann.co.uk/library
Visit our website to find out more information about
Heinemann Library books.

To order:
☎ Phone 44 (0) 1865 888066
▤ Send a fax to 44 (0) 1865 314091
▯ Visit the Heinemann Bookshop at
www.heinemann.co.uk/library to browse our catalogue and
order online.

First published in Great Britain by
Heinemann Library, Halley Court, Jordan
Hill, Oxford
OX2 8EJ, part of Harcourt Education.
Heinemann is a registered trademark of
Harcourt Education Ltd.

© Harcourt Education Ltd 2005
First published in paperback in 2006
The moral right of the proprietor has been
asserted.

Editors: Nancy Dickmann and Sarah
Chappelow
Design: Ron Kamen and
       Dave Oakley/Arnos Design
Illustrations: Barry Atkinson
Maps: Jeff Edwards
Picture Researcher: Erica Newbery
       and Elaine Willis
Production Controller: Camilla Smith

Originated by Modern Age
Printed and bound in China
by WKT Company Limited

10 dig ISBN 0 431 04294 2 (hardback)
13 dig ISBN 978 0431 042947
09 08 07 06 05
10 9 8 7 6 5 4 3 2 1

10 dig ISBN 0 431 04299 3 (paperback)
13 dig ISBN 978 0431 042992
10 09 08 07 06
10 9 8 7 6 5 4 3 2 1

British Library Cataloguing in Publication
Data
Shuter, Jane
Life in ancient Athens. - (Picture the past)
938.5
A full catalogue record for this book is
available from the British Library.

Acknowledgements:
The publishers would like to thank the
following for permission to reproduce
photographs: AAAC p. **24**; AKG pp. **8**, **23**
(Erich Lessing), **28** (John Hios); Art Archive
pp. **14** (Dagli Orti), **19**, **25** (Kanellopoulus
Museum, Athens/Dagli Orti), **26** (Dagli
Orti); Bildarchiv Preussischer Kulturbesitz p.
22; Bridgeman pp. **10** (Lauros/Giraudon),
16 (Lauros/Giraudon), **21** (British Museum);
Corbis pp. **6** (James Davis/Eye Ubiquitous),
12 (Charles O'Rear); Richard Butcher &
Magnet Harlequin p. **13** (Harcourt
Education Ltd); Scala p. **18** (Louvre, Paris);
Werner Forman p. **20**.

Cover photograph of a bowl showing the
daily activities of people living in ancient
Athens reproduced with permission on
Topham.

Every effort has been made to contact
copyright holders of any material
reproduced in this book. Any omissions will
be rectified in subsequent printings if
notice is given to the publishers.

Contents

Any words appearing in bold, **like this**, are explained in the Glossary.

Who were the ancient Greeks?

All the people who lived in ancient Greece spoke the same language and **worshipped** the same gods and goddesses. But they all lived in different **city states** – a city and the land around it that it controlled. These city states were all run differently, and there were often fights between them. Despite this, there were things that were the same in the city states. Because they had the same religion, they shared big **religious festivals**. They also joined together to fight attackers from outside Greece.

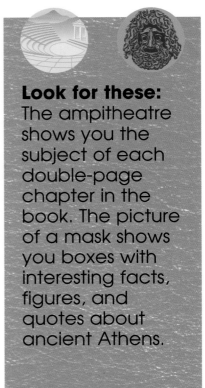

Look for these:
The ampitheatre shows you the subject of each double-page chapter in the book. The picture of a mask shows you boxes with interesting facts, figures, and quotes about ancient Athens.

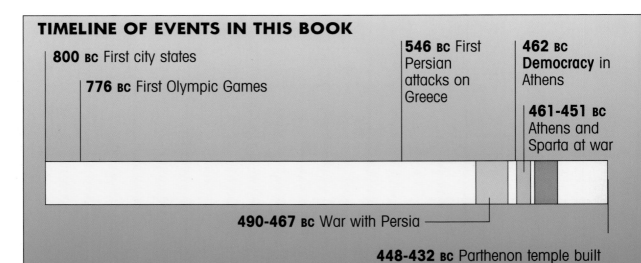

TIMELINE OF EVENTS IN THIS BOOK

800 BC First city states

776 BC First Olympic Games

546 BC First Persian attacks on Greece

462 BC **Democracy** in Athens

461-451 BC Athens and Sparta at war

490-467 BC War with Persia

448-432 BC Parthenon temple built for goddess Athena in Athens

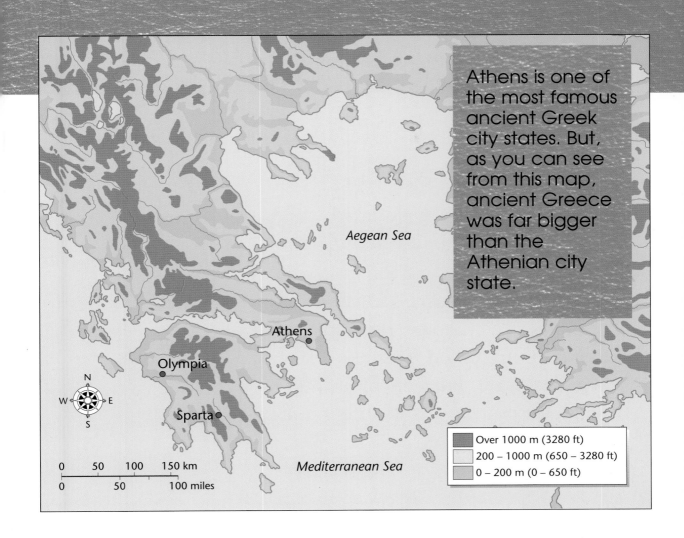

Athens is one of the most famous ancient Greek city states. But, as you can see from this map, ancient Greece was far bigger than the Athenian city state.

Aegean Sea

Athens

Olympia

Sparta

Mediterranean Sea

| 0 | 50 | 100 | 150 km |
| 0 | | 50 | 100 miles |

Over 1000 m (3280 ft)
200 – 1000 m (650 – 3280 ft)
0 – 200 m (0 – 650 ft)

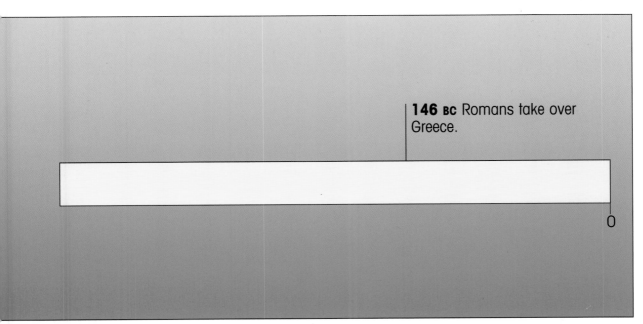

146 BC Romans take over Greece.

0

The city state

Some **city states** had fewer than a thousand **citizens**. Others, like Athens and Sparta, were much bigger. The whole city state was run from the city itself. But the land all around was important, too. The farmers that worked on this land had to grow enough food to feed everyone in the city state. Farmers mainly lived in villages, but those with the biggest farms sometimes lived in a farmhouse on their land.

The Greek mountains and the sea divided ancient Greece up into areas that often became separate city states.

Farmers worked in similar ways all over Greece, no matter which city state they lived in. They wanted to use as much of the land as they could, even in difficult places. They built 'steps' up steep hillsides, making thin strips of flat land to grow crops on. Farmers grew grain and vegetables. On land where the soil was not rich enough to grow other crops, they grew olive trees. They used simple wooden tools.

City states were run in different ways. In Athens, all **citizens** had the same rights. The Athenians ran their city state as a **democracy**. This meant that all male citizens could vote on what to do. Sparta was not run as a democracy. The Spartans had a huge number of **slaves** in their city state, and lived in fear of a slave **revolt**. So a few important citizens ran their city state, following a strict set of rules. To them, the most important thing was to produce brave Spartan soldiers, to fight other city states and control the slaves.

Athenians voted on things by putting up their hands. Sometimes, however, they voted using ballots, like the ones shown here, or pieces of pottery. These were collected in and added up to find out how people had voted.

Not everyone in Athens took part in the system of democracy. Women, children, slaves, and **foreigners** living in Athens were not allowed to vote. That left about 40,000 male citizens who could vote. Not everyone did. Men who lived far outside the city seldom came to vote. But no decision could be made until at least 6,000 men were at a **debate**.

This picture shows an artist's idea of Athenians meeting to vote. Usually an important citizen suggested a new law, or maybe going to war. Once he had spoken, every man who was there could say what he thought. After this debate, the citzens voted.

Athens

Athens had different kinds of **citizens** – rich, poor, and many levels in between. The Athenians were proud of their city and spent a lot of money on the **public buildings** there. Rich citizens happily gave money to build a new **temple**, or improve the **agora** – the main square. They spent a lot of time in the agora, talking, arranging marriages, and listening to people giving speeches. **Traders** set up their stalls all around the agora.

DIFFERENT CITIES

Unlike the Athenians, the Spartans were not interested in building beautiful cities. Thucydides, an Athenian writer, said in about 420 BC, "If Sparta were deserted, visitors looking at its remains would not know how powerful it had been. If Athens were deserted, visitors looking at its remains would think it had been twice as great as it is."

Athens sold its **goods** to other places. This is called trade. It was one of the ways that Athens became rich. People wanted Athenian jars, like this one, because they were so beautifully made.

The public buildings of Athens were large and made from stone. Athenian homes were small and made from mud brick. Several visitors to Athens in ancient times wrote about how small the houses of ordinary people were. These homes crowded together along twisting streets. The streets were just dirt and were covered with the rubbish people threw out every day.

Temples and religion

The ancient Greeks believed in many different gods and goddesses who could affect everyday life. The gods had to be kept happy, so the ancient Greeks **worshipped** them and built them beautiful **temples**. These temples were homes for the gods – ordinary people did not go into them. They prayed to small statues of the gods in their homes or by the roadside.

THE GODS

The ancient Greeks believed the twelve most important gods and goddesses lived as a family. Zeus was the father of the gods and his wife, Hera, was the goddess of marriage. The brothers and children of Zeus were called Hades, Persephone, Poseidon, Demeter, Aphrodite, Athena, Apollo, Artemis, Ares, and Hephaestus. Sometimes, the gods Hermes and Dionysus are included in this family too.

The biggest temple in Athens is the Parthenon, a temple for the city's special goddess, Athena.

The ancient Greeks held **religious festivals** for their gods and goddesses. They could go on for several days. There were dozens of big festivals each year. Different parts of Greece also had smaller festivals for less important gods.

The people in each city state thought one god or goddess took special care of them. Athenians told how the god Poseidon and the goddess Athena fought over which of them would protect Athens. Athena won.

In the story of how Poseidon and Athena fought over Athens, an olive tree grew on a spot where Athena's spear landed. Some people say that the olive tree in this picture, which is in the same place as the tree in the story, grew from a shoot of that first tree.

Theatres

Plays were put on in ancient Greek theatres as part of **religious festivals**, to entertain the gods. They were not put on just as entertainment. Ordinary people went to watch the plays, which were either funny comedies or tragedies where things usually turned out badly. We do not know if women went. If they went they sat in a different part of the theatre from the men. The **priests** who worked in the temples looking after the gods sat at the front.

The masks that actors wore were often used to decorate public buildings, such as temples. This broken piece of roof decoration shows three different kinds of masks.

All actors were men. They wore masks to show if they were old or young, happy or sad, and male or female characters. There was a group of about a dozen people called the chorus. They told the story, sang, danced, and made comments on what was happening. The actors stood on the stage and spoke their lines.

This picture shows an artist's idea of a play being performed in ancient Greek times. The actors in the semi-circle below the stage are the chorus.

Shopping

The ancient Greeks did most of their shopping at markets. The markets in Athens were held in the main square, the **agora**. People sold vegetables, cheese, and wine from covered stalls. Poorer people sold their vegetables or other **goods** from mats on the ground. People also bought goods such as vases, shoes, and furniture from the workshops where they were made.

This young man is making a helmet. More tools hang on a rack behind his head.

WHO WENT SHOPPING?

Men did the shopping in ancient Greece. This is because women were expected to stay at home. Women from poorer families went shopping or sold things at markets. But it was seen as something women only did if they had to.

A **craftsman**, or a group of craftsmen, ran a workshop. Most workshops had around eight to ten people working in them. There were usually a skilled craftsman, three or four **slaves**, and several boys and young men learning the craft.

Shoppers often visited pottery workshops like this one. Workshops needed workers with several different skills. In this workshop, they have potters to make the pots and artists to paint them, as well as other workers to fetch and carry.

Work

In cities such as Athens, there were many small workshops making many different things such as shoes, furniture, clothes, cooking pots, and jewellery. There was a sword maker in Athens who had over 30 slaves and probably about 20 other workers. This was a very big workshop. People also found work building and repairing homes, or moving goods from one part of the city to the other.

SPECIALIZATION

Specialization is making just one thing. One Athenian thinker said, "In a small **city state** one man makes beds, doors, ploughs, tables, and even builds homes. He cannot be good at all these jobs. In a large city state a man can make just beds and do it very well."

Many Greek farmers made their own wine. They drank some and took the rest to the city market, by cart, to sell.

Women and very young children did not work unless their families were really poor or farmers. On farms, everyone worked at busy times of the year, such as harvest time. It was very important to collect the crops quickly, before they got too ripe or were spoiled by bad weather.

Some workshops made beautifully decorated goods, like the vase on page 10. Others made simple cooking pots, like this one, for everyday use.

Family life

In Athens, families were important. Parents arranged marriages for their children. The couple often did not meet until their wedding day. Women lived by themselves with their children and **slaves**, in rooms at the back of the house or upstairs. In the tiny homes of the poorer parts of Athens this was not possible. Women had to avoid men from outside their own families as much as they could.

NO CHOICE

A woman in a play by Sophocles, a famous Greek **playwright**, says, "We are sold away from our home. Some go to the home of strangers. Some go to joyless homes, other to ones where they are disliked. And all this, once we have been married, we have to praise."

Women were expected to start having babies as soon as possible after they got married. If possible, they had a nursemaid (a sort of nanny) to help to bring them up.

Men often held dinner parties for each other. The only women allowed at these were female entertainers who danced and played music.

Most families, except for the poorest, had at least one slave to do the hardest work around the house. Slaves were servants who were bought and sold, just like **goods**. They had to work very hard for the person who owned them. Most slaves were **foreigners**, though a few came from other parts of Greece.

Education

In Athens, and most of the other **city states**, education for boys was important. Education had to be paid for, so boys from rich families went to the best schools. They also stayed at school for longer. From the age of seven, boys learned to read aloud, recite from memory, and write. They also had to learn how to wrestle – they needed to be fit to fight for the city state.

The first ancient Greeks wrote on wooden boards covered with wax. They pressed the letters into the wax with a pointed stylus. Later Greeks used paper and ink.

SPARTAN EDUCATION

Spartan boys left home at seven years old to live in large groups. They learned to read and write, but mostly trained to be good soldiers. They were fed very little so they would be hungry enough to go hunting more food. Their rooms were bare. They were only given two pieces of clothing a year.

Rather than going to school, some boys went straight to workshops to learn a **trade**. Others were taught basic reading and writing and then went to learn a trade. Richer boys learned to write poetry and **debate** with each other. They also learned to make speeches. This was an important skill for the sons of wealthy **citizens**. They would be expected to take part in the city's debates.

Girls were taught to run a home. If they were poor they learned to cook, sew, and weave cloth. Girls from rich families learned how to run a house full of servants.

Transport

Most people did not travel far in ancient Greece. The mountains made travel difficult and most roads were just narrow dirt paths. But people travelled from all over Greece for the biggest Greek **religious festival**, the Olympic Games. These were held at Olympia every four years. To compete in or to watch these Games, people walked or travelled by cart or donkey.

SENDING MESSAGES

There was no postal service in ancient Greece. People wrote a message for a messenger to deliver. These messengers walked. Sometimes people just told the messenger what they wanted to say and hoped he would remember!

Because mountains made travelling on land difficult, the ancient Greeks travelled by sea whenever they could.

Walking was the way for everyone, rich and poor, to get around. People walked around cities like Athens and they also walked to nearby villages. A rich person took a slave with him, to carry his things. Because they took regular exercise, most Athenian men were fit. They did not find walking long distances a problem.

As well as using carts to carry heavy things, the ancient Greeks also enjoyed racing them. Exciting and dangerous races were held using small carts, called chariots, pulled by fast horses.

Health and food

The ancient Greeks, no matter how rich they were, ate very little meat. They ate bread, porridge, fish, cheese, butter, vegetables, and fruit. Meat was mostly eaten at **sacrifices** during **religious festivals**. Doctors said men needed to eat well and take lots of exercise to stay healthy. They did not think women needed as much exercise. But the Spartans believed that women should exercise to be healthy mothers.

WINE

Everyone drank wine in ancient Greece, even children! But they all drank it watered down. Children had it mixed with a lot of water. Grown men also added water to wine, but in small amounts. They thought it was bad manners to drink unwatered wine.

Doctors gave advice about keeping healthy and cared for the sick. They also operated on people when they had to.

Honey fritters

The ancient Greeks ate carefully, but still enjoyed treats, like pastries sweetened with lots of honey. Sweet and savoury things were both cooked in olive oil, like the sweet fritters here.

WARNING: do not cook anything unless there is an adult to help you. You may need them to do the frying for you.

You will need:
100g (4 oz) plain flour
150ml (1/3 pint) of water
2 tablespoons of honey
1 teaspoon of sesame seeds
oil for frying

1 Slowly add the water to the flour in a bowl, stirring as you add it so it does not go lumpy.

2 Stir in a spoonful of honey.

3 Heat 2 spoons of oil on a medium heat in a frying pan. Pour in 1/4 of the mixture when the oil is hot.

4 Wait until the mixture thickens, then turn it over. Do this two or three times, until the fritter is brown on both sides.

5 Make 3 more fritters in the same way.

6 Pour the rest of the honey over them and sprinkle with sesame seeds.

War

The ancient Greeks were often at war. **City states** fought each other. Sometimes city states that were enemies joined together to fight against **foreigners**. All the men in a city state were expected to fight if they could, no matter how old they were. They had to train to be ready to fight. They had to bring their own **armour** and weapons.

FIGHTING SEASONS

Sea battles mostly took place between April and October, because of the weather. Land battles were often in the spring and summer – winter weather made fighting difficult. People tried not to fight in autumn as this was the main harvest time. If all the men were away fighting, the crops might rot in the fields.

Spartan warriors wore long red cloaks and helmets, but often fought naked. They thought this made them look brave and frightened the enemy. Also, they had discovered that wounds did not heal well when covered by cloth.

Athens became powerful because of its **navy**, which fought at sea. At first, the Greeks used to sail close enough to each other for the men on board to fight. Then they put a large metal ram on the front of their ships. They sailed straight at enemy ships, hoping to make a hole in the ship and sink it, leaving the men on board to drown.

This picture by a modern artist shows Greek soldiers on the left fighting the Persians on the right.

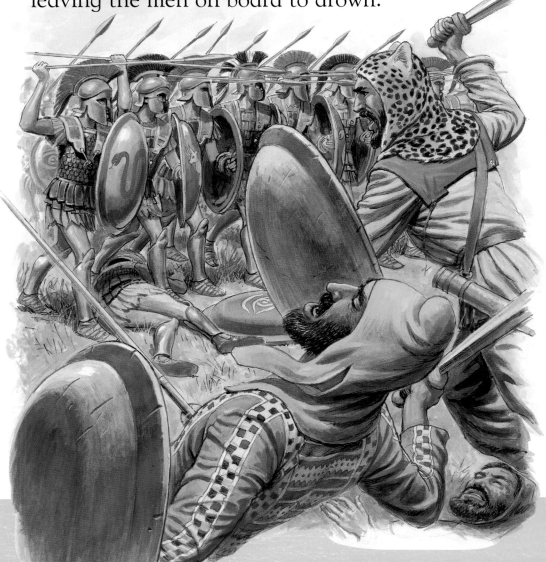

29

Glossary

agora open space, often near the centre of a town, with public buildings and shops around it. It was often used as a meeting place.

armour covering, often of metal, made to protect soldiers' bodies in battle

citizen man who is born in a city to parents who were citizens. Citizens had rights in their own city that they would not have had in any other.

city state a city and the land it controls around it

craftsman men who have been specially trained to make things

debate argument, in front of an audience, about a question or idea. In a debate, people had to argue well and the audience decided who had won.

democracy "rule by the people"; this is when at least some ordinary people get to take part in running the country

foreigner person who comes from one country to visit, or live in, another country. Foreigners often speak a different language.

goods things that are made, bought, and sold

navy ships used to fight for a country

playwright person who writes plays to be performed in a theatre

priest (priestess) man (or woman) who works in a temple serving a god or goddess

public building building that is used by everyone in a town or city, or one that the town or city is run from

religious festival several days of religious ceremonies, held every year

revolt when a group of people in a country act against the people running the country. Revolts are often violent.

sacrifice something given to a god or a goddess as a gift

slave person who is bought and sold by someone, to work for that person

temple place where gods and goddesses are worshipped

trade this can mean:
1 a job
2 selling or swapping goods

worship when a god or goddess is praised or shown respect

Further resources

Books

Ancient Greece, Christine Hatt (Heinemann Library, 2004)
Explore History: Ancient Greece (Heinemann Library, 2001)
History in Art: Ancient Greece, Andrew Langley (Raintree, 2004)
The Ancient Greeks, Pat Taylor (Heinemann Library, 1994)
What families were like: Ancient Greece, Alison Cooper
(Hodder Wayland, 2001)
Worldwise: Ancient Greeks, Daisy Kerr (Franklin Watts, 1997)
You are in Ancient Greece, Ivan Minnis (Raintree, 2004)

Websites

www.ancientgreece.com
A good website looking at all aspects of ancient Greek life.

www.historyforkids.org/learn/greeks
A useful website full of links and extra resources.

www.bbc.co.uk/schools/ancientgreece/main_menu.shtml
Use the games and interactive activities to find out more
about life in ancient Greece.

www.olympic.org/uk/games/ancient/index_uk.asp
Visit this website to find out all about the Olympics.

Index